Wildest Dreams2

Book #2 of the Wildest Dreams Series

By Michael Young

Royal Media and Publishing
P. O. Box 4321
Jeffersonville, IN 47131
502-802-5385
http://royalmediaandpublishing.com
royalmediapublishing@gmail.com

Cover Design: Elite Covers

ISBN-13: 978-1-955501-01-9

Printed in the United States of America

Dedication

This book is dedicated to my grandmother, Virginia Young who sparked my love of books.

Acknowledgements

I wish to acknowledge my fans for encouraging and supporting me as I bring them original and unique story telling.

Michael A. Young

Table of Contents

Introduction

The phrase "love you to death" is a very common thing people say to each other. Usually, it means that someone has a love so deep for another that it will last until the other passes away. If you think of it that way, it's very sweet and enduring. As previously said, this phrase is usually and commonly used in this way.

Although it can be, and sometimes is, used as a loving phrase, but with a dark, very dark, undertone. When someone says it and subconsciously means death more than the love, well, you are dealing with a very dangerous person. When they say, "love you to death," they really mean it. If they can't love you, no one will!

So beware and take care when you hear "love you to death" because that person just may mean it… literally!

Chapter 1

Say That Again

The music blared and the strobe lights swung around the club, shining on club patrons on the dance floor and some standing at the bar. Quite a few were standing grouped together with concern on their faces. Here and there in the crowd, if you were close enough, you could hear a few people conversing with each, discussing what they had just seen.

"Oh my God! Is she all right?"

"I think she may be drunk and fell."

"I saw her and that guy with her arguing. He hit her when the guy in the suit walked up. Damn shame."

With all the people around, you would think at least one person would get the story right, but people will think they saw one thing when, actually, something totally different happened. Just like what happened here in the club.

"Shanette! Shanette! Are you all right? Somebody… please get somebody, please help us!"

Sitting on the club floor with her head on his legs, Scott Mozell held Shanette's hand with one of his while pressing a wet cloth a bartender had given him on her forehead.

Slowly, she came back around, blinking her eyes, trying to focus on anything. Looking up at Scott's face with that concerned look on it, she cracked a small smile. Squeezing his hand, she pulled it close and kissed it. Her attention was drawn to a figure standing over Scott's shoulder. A face. A somewhat familiar face. As she focused more, the face wasn't somewhat, it was damn sure.

Sitting up and putting her hand against Scott's chest, she looked at the man standing over them smiling.

"How in the hell can this be? Tell me how the hell you… just how the fuck?"

"Shanette, do you know this guy?"

Stuttering with tears in her eyes, she stood, eyes still locked on the well-dressed gentleman. Scott held her steady until she got her balance.

"Regal. His name is Regal, Scott. Remember, I was telling you about the guy in my life who was killed? We are looking at him right now."

"But how? You said... How? No fucking way, this can't be him. This can't be the Regal guy who died. Sorry, honey, you must be mistaken."

"Scott, is it? Ms. Tolls is right. I am Mr. Regal, but she is also wrong."

The two looked at Regal, then at each other, and then back at Regal. In unison, they both asked, "WRONG?"

"Yes, I am not the Regal whom Ms. Tolls is speaking of. I am his brother, twin brother, Alondo. I have been out of the country for some time now. Anthony probably never mentioned me."

On her feet now and calming down, a sense of reality settled over Shanette. Taking a few steps closer, she took a hard look at Alondo. "Oh my god! You are an exact mirror image of Anthony. Except for, naturally, the facial hair... and something about the eyes. Although they seem to be the same color, there is definitely a difference."

"In my opinion, I think I'm slightly better looking, being more mature by seven minutes." As Alondo began to chuckle, Scott also cracked a smile at the joke, feeling relieved that this man wasn't Shanette's ex love interest.

While Shanette was still in awe of the resemblance, Scott broke the weird tension by reaching out to shake hands and introduce himself, "Alondo, my name is Scott Mozell. I'm an old, old friend of Shanette's, going back to late high school years."

"Pleasure to meet you, Scott."

Rejoining the conversation, Shanette apologized for not introducing Scott then asked Alondo a question, "You said out of town? Where were you that you couldn't be here for your brother's funeral?"

"Not just out of town, out of the country. Italy, as a matter of fact, taking care of some personal financial obligations. Anthony and I haven't actually been on very good terms in a long time, as in haven't spoken in quite a while, a very long while. The news just recently came to me of my brother's death, or better said, murder."

As Alondo spoke of murder, a look came across his face that wasn't sadness, but more of anger. Shanette finally reached out and held his hand, trying to show some sort of compassion. He used his other hand and laid it onto hers then smiled. As they continued to converse, he told them a mutual friend of his and his brother's told him about the passing and the woman in his brother's life, and also said the club, or at her job at the agency, would be the best places to find her. He'd just arrived in town a couple hours before, so if she wasn't at the club, he had planned to try her workplace tomorrow.

"My dear and good fellow, I must ask your forgiveness, for I am extremely tired from the flight and time changes. I will be in town for a short period of time, and I will do my best to meet up with you both again."

Shanette hugged him and said, "Sure, anytime."

Scott patted his shoulder and said, "No problem."

Alondo left the club and immediately took out a handkerchief and wiped his hands. "Filthy, vile bitch. You'll definitely be seeing me again, and you will pay for being involved in Anthony's death!" Then he tossed the handkerchief away as he called for a taxi and was driven away.

Chapter 2

What about Anthony?

Sitting on the couch, with her head on Scott's chest while watching TV, Shanette's mind danced around, thinking about Alondo and Anthony. What could have had him gone so long that he was unaware of his only brother's death? Was Anthony truly his only brother? Could there be more out there? The question of whether he really was his brother was undeniable. They looked exactly alike. There was something about Alondo's eyes, though, that bothered her, something behind them, pain, remorse, anger…

"Shanette! Shanette! Did you hear me?"

"Huh, what? What did you say, Scott?"

"I asked if you are all right?"

"Yes, why?"

"Your ex-boyfriend's brother, who looks just like him, has shown up out of nowhere. That had to have had some sort of effect on you."

"Honestly, it did. I was just lying here thinking about it. What happened between them, for Alondo not to keep in touch with Anthony? He had to find out everything from an assistant."

"Well, what type of man was his brother Anthony? Alondo seems pretty smooth."

Shanette sat up and leaned back against the arm of the couch. It has been a while since she had spoken of Regal, but the memories were still fresh in her mind.

"Well, Anthony wasn't officially a boyfriend. We only had sex once…and that was in a dream that Dominece rudely woke me from—"

"Rudely? Sounds like Dom all right."

"He was more than a friend, but not a lover per se. If that makes any sense. He was a special friend with boyfriend potential. He was a very kind and understanding man. My friends thought he was a great guy. Even brother Gerald liked him. They even had a few business ventures together. Personality wise, he was a lot like you, Scott, a self-made man, with high moral values."

Leaning over to reach for a bottle of beer sitting on the table, Scott took a sip and smiled. "Well, this Anthony sounds like a real good, genuine guy. Especially if he had brother Gerald's seal of approval, and you know how he feels about you girls—very protective."

Grabbing her beer and following Scott's lead, she drank from her own bottle. "Hell yeah. The only other guy Gerald would relax around was you. Always did. He would say if he couldn't be there, Scott had better be."

"Speaking of him, I need to get at G, but back to Mr. Regal. If he didn't pass, I'm sure you two would have become an amazing couple."

"Possibly, but you and I wouldn't be in each other's lives again."

"That's not true. We would have run into each other again and kicked it as friends."

"Maybe, but not friends who chill in each other's arms and kiss."

"That's true." Then Scott pulled her close and kissed her.

Chapter 3

More In Play Than You Know

Alondo sat in a coffee shop making faces as he sipped on a drink he thought was far less than adequate. Overseas, even the worst morning brew was better than this so called "most requested" dark roasted trash juice. Oh, how he missed life out of the country. If he could have helped it, this trip back home would've never happened, but the death of Anthony and his involvement with that whore Shanette demanded attention.

Unable to swallow any more of the dreadful piss, he checked the time on his watch and looked toward the door. Like clockwork, Danny Meek came in and took a seat. Shortly after, T'ondra Dove entered with her friend and accountant Andrea Koss.

"I guess the information was worth the money, Mr. Flose." Alondo crossed his legs and opened a paper to hide the fact he was watching T'ondra.

After the meeting, the group split and went their separate ways. Andrea Koss stayed behind and finished her beverage.

Before she got up, Alondo smoothly walked over and spoke. "Excuse me, Ms., please forgive this intrusion. My name is Alondo Regal."

"Hello, Mr. Regal. How can I help you?"

"Actually, it's more like how I can help you."

Frowning, she asked, "Say what? Help me? How is that?" Then she slid her chair back to get up.

"Well, it's more like how I can help Ms. Dove!"

Andrea slowly sat back down and gave Alondo a confused look, never taking her eyes off his. "How do you know Ms. Dove? I know everyone she knows, and, sir, I don't fucking know you! My time is precious and short. Ms. Dove's time is more so. We don't have time for would-be, wanna-be directors, producers, or anyone wanting her to represent some bullshit ass product—"

"Let me stop you right there. I am none of the above. I come from money, old money, as you can tell by my attire. I don't need her or you, to further my fortune. What I can provide is her spark back."

"Spark back?"

"Yes, spark, as in Mr. Mozell. I know he was the motivation that briefly put her back in the conversation of the entertainment world, and after he chose another woman, she faded back into the shadows."

Falling back in her chair, she was amazed. The amount of personal information this man knew about T'ondra blew her mind. She wanted to ask how he knew so much, but he had given her his answer in advance. He came from old money, and old money bought a lot. "Mr. Regal, what is it you want?"

Leaning forward, his look never changed. It wasn't a stern look, but there was nothing soft in it, either. His look was that of confidence and power. "Ms. Koss, all I want is to give Ms. Dove her edge of power back. I'm all about power."

"How do you know me? Never mind. Old money."

"That's right. Old money is power, my dear, and power affords you many things, like information."

The two continued to talk for a while, with Alondo never once changing positions in his seat, but Andrea wiggled and squirmed with discomfort. How did he know so much and how would he be able to do what he proposed? Andrea was in mid-sentence when Alondo glanced at his watch and interrupted her, "Ms. Koss, please relay our conversation to Ms. Dove if you will."

"Ahh, okay. I'm not sure if it is something she would want, but I—"

"It's not a request. Tell her, and after she agrees, I will be in touch with her. Hopefully this will be our last interaction, for we won't have a use for an in-between person anymore." Leaving a gold-plated business card on the table, he adjusted his suit coat, then turned and walked out the cafe' without another word.

***

Looking at the metal card as she picked it up, she saw that it read, *Alondo Regal, C.E.O., Regal Financial Investing and Trading*. Koss thought, *what an arrogant asshole*, but he was damn attractive and he knew it. Flipping the card over and over in her fingers, she got up and dialed T'ondra as she left the cafe'. "Bitch, I may have a way for you to get back on track again and get some good dick back in your life."

Chapter 4

Mr. Charming

The crowd in the black glass tower that was home to the Donovan Agency buzzed around like lost worker bees. Beautiful women and handsome men eyed each other in passing, but time for flirting and hookups must wait because time, to people downtown, was very important and valuable. The security guard, on the other hand, was throwing out dirty comments to women like a person passing bad checks.

"Hey, sexy brown cinnamon! Yeah, you in that tight cream-colored skirt. Girl, you coming through like a young stallion."

The woman rolled her eyes at him as she passed, when her gaze caught a well-dressed man coming through the turnstile. He paid little attention to the passers-by, especially the men. He walked with an amazing confidence, not of a man who owned a business, but that of a man who owned a couple of buildings, also sensing that, because he was an alpha, other men gave him plenty of space as he stepped through. Even the security guard stopped flirting with the women when he approached, figuring he was someone very important, with the influence to get him fired.

"Sir, you need any help finding your destination?"

Stopping in front of securities desk, he straightened his tie and placed his hands behind his back. "Yes, actually, you can, and it will save me valuable time. Where can I find the Donovan Agency?"

The guard directed him to an elevator and told him which floor to go to, then the guy walked away without another look or even a thank you. As the guard moved on, he spoke about the man under his breath. "Arrogant bastard," he said.

A woman close by, who was admiring the guy, overheard him and replied, "That man there isn't arrogant! He's someone oozing confidence and sexuality."

***

The doors opened up and Alondo stepped out. His eyes scanned the area. *Not bad*, he thought, *plenty of people working, beautiful women everywhere, and it's freaking huge in here. This place could possibly be a huge money maker.*

Maybe he should buy it. His eyes locked on a familiar face coming from an office near the back—that bitch, Shanette Tolls.

A man with an accent approached him. "Excuse me, sir, may I assist you?" Then he paused and stared, wide-eyed.

Looking the older gentleman over, Alondo noticed he was well dressed. Not as nice as himself, but nice nonetheless.

"Yes, yes, you can. Can you let Ms. Shanette Tolls know that Regal has stopped by to see her?"

Still with a shocked look on his face, he murmured an answer, "Regal? Anthony Regal? I thought… we thought… you're supposed to be…"

Reaching out to shake the guy's hand, he introduced himself, "Alondo, Alondo Regal. Anthony was my twin brother."

With the look of shame mixed with relief that he wasn't seeing a ghost, the older man shook the hand in front of him. "Please forgive my rudeness and insensitivity. My name is Jack Arms, a business associate of Shanette's. Just a second. I believe she is in a meeting, but it should be concluding soon."

Jack led Alondo toward a waiting area, but Shanette approached before they reached it. She shook Jack's shoulders and hugged him from behind, telling him that Toni and Vikki were waiting to go to lunch, and if he wanted to go to bring his narrow behind on. Jack told Alondo his goodbye pleasantries, stuck his tongue out at Shanette and trotted off, holding his narrow butt.

"Ms. Tolls, once again, it's a pleasure to be in your company. Please forgive the intrusion, but I needed to ask something concerning my late brother."

"Sure, Alondo, anything you need to know, go ahead and ask."

"Ms. Tolls, I would be honored if you'd let me treat you to lunch so we can have a more private conversation."

"Alondo, you are in luck. I just finished a stressful meeting, and a break from this atmosphere is just what I need. Give me three minutes to get my purse, and we can go."

"Ms. Tolls, the lunch is on me so you can leave your things here."

"Thank you, but a woman is always prepared, just in case the 'just in case' happens."

In his mind, he applauded her. Very good thinking, young lady, very good. "I'll be right here, and since this is your city, I'll be relying on you to pick our dining spot."

"I think I know a place that will do just fine, trust me."

"All right." In his head, he said, *Trust you? Anthony trusted you, and look where that led him, bitch.*

Chapter 5

Shouldn't Surprise Anymore

Andrea Koss sat at a red light, tapping her hand on the steering wheel while listening to the radio. The proposal Alondo Regal had for T'ondra was absolutely insane. There was no way in a frozen hell that it could possibly work, his claims to be able to do the impossible, the unbelievable. T' had tried some stupid shit in the past, but this! This probably would be right up her alley. No harm in telling her, what she did after that was on her.

Andrea pulled up to T'ondra's home and got out, looking around. Noticing another car in the driveway off to the side, she made her way to the backyard. The once lovely home that was renovated by Scott Mozell's company was now a shadow of itself. The pool, which was enlarged and had a bar and hot tub added, now was debris-filled and not quite blue, but bluish green. Inside, the walls and cabinets were damaged due to a drunken rage after numerous failed endeavors after Scott and T' ended.

"Yo, T'. Where are you?" Walking around and coming in the house, Andrea continued to call for her friend and client. "T'ondra, where the hell you at?"

Hearing some voices coming from upstairs, she made her way up and went into the bedroom. The voices got a little louder, but she couldn't understand what was being said.

"Hey, T'on—"

There, in the middle of the master bathroom, was T'ondra, standing naked with a young woman on her knees and her mouth between her thighs. Also, there was a young man on his knees, with his face buried in T'ondra's ass. She had been doing some crazy shit, but who in the hell were these two people with mouths full of Dove.

"T'ondra, what the fuck!"

Not even looking toward Andrea, T'ondra stood there with her head thrown back in pure ecstasy. As the duo of tongues delighted her body, she caressed her still wet breasts and nipples. She moaned the words "more" and "faster" to the two, then she opened her eyes and glanced over to see her best friend and accountant, Andrea, in the doorway with her mouth open and a very shocked look on her face.

"Hey, girl. What's up?"

The guy and girl removed their faces and mouths from the secret places. The woman fell back on her ass and scrambled to find something to cover up with. The guy jumped up and stood next to T'. His penis was still hard and strong, and from Andrea's vantage point, it looked like he was a good foot away from T' and that monster of a cock was still touching her thigh.

"You two can go now. Thank you for the tongue play. Maybe next time, I'll let you use that dragon tail between your legs on me... maybe."

"Yes, Ms. Dove. It was a pleasure to meet you, and my wife and I had an amazing time." They dressed quickly and left the room. Shortly after, the front door opened and closed.

***

"Before you ask, I met them at a club last night. They talked about me being a sex symbol, and her catching him masturbating to my movies, and him saying his wife said if she did get down with a woman, it would be with me. So blah blah blah, I gave them a treat."

"Bitch, you're a straight freak and whore."

"Maybe, but I'm not a horny one anymore."

Dove got dressed and they went downstairs into the lounge, which was a room with several love seats and lounge chairs and a large TV on one side and a huge stereo and speakers on the other. Andrea told T'ondra about Alondo and the plan he had for her, but that she had to meet him in person to discuss it. Once she heard the name Scott Mozell, Dove was all for the meeting.

Chapter 6

Getting To Know Regal

A waitress set two plates down on a table then flashed a smile before walking away. The pair at the table dove into their food, their utensils flashing under the lights in the restaurant. Not much was said as the two enjoyed the meals on their plates. The waitress returned and asked if the food tasted all right and if they needed anything.

The guy glanced up at her and rudely commented, "If we need anything, one of us will let you know. Thank you!"

Taken aback, the waitress took a step backwards.

"Not right now, thank you. Everything is great, wonderful."

The waitress smiled back at the lady patron and told her if they needed anything to please let her know. Then she left to take care of another table.

Looking over at her table mate, Shanette gave him a look of anger mixed with embarrassment. "Alondo. Don't you think that was a tad bit rude?"

Looking over at her, he gave her a cold, icy glare, then it softened as he spoke. "Forgive me, my dear, for my bluntness. I have been accustomed to the type of service overseas where the servers treat you like, for a better lack of wording, shit. I will make amends with the young lady on her next passing."

"I see. I can't imagine how different the two cultures must be. Has it been difficult for you getting used to things over here again?"

"Somewhat. There are rude, obnoxious people no matter where you go. It's the way you deal with them that's important. I just give them back what they give me."

"Really? How do they respond to that type of treatment?"

With a sort of sinister smile, he replied, "Who cares?"

The waitress came close by again. Alondo reached out and touched her arm to get her attention.

"Yes, sir, is everything okay? What can I get for you?"

"All is well, my dear. I would like to ask your forgiveness for my rude behavior previously."

"Sir, no worries. No harm done, no offense taken. Be sure to let me know if there is anything I can get you."

Shanette looked at Alondo and smiled before taking another bite of food.

What she had no idea of was that the apology felt like a burning, jagged knife being slowly shoved into his spine. If he had to lower himself to another one of these low life, snail trail simpletons, he might just implode. Alondo held himself superior to most… well… everyone. Being here in this eatery, served by insufferable human waste and sharing a less than subpar meal with a vile, murderous winch… Unable to stomach any more of the whole situation, he decided to get to the point of this meeting. "Ms. Tolls. How exactly did you and my brother meet?"

Shanette took a sip from her glass and told him everything from being hired by him to sitting at his funeral. Saddened by reminiscing of Anthony, but no longer brought to tears, she sat and looked at him with warm eyes.

"I also learned of him leaving you the club. I'll bet that acquisition is providing you with some serious returns, I mean, more than that office job of yours."

Shocked by his bluntness and utter rudeness, she answered in a manner in which he would be accustomed, "First off, no, he didn't leave me ownership of the club, only free access for me and my friends, thanks to the manager. The only thing I was left with was a broken heart—"

Alondo cut her off by saying, "So you were expecting some kind of financial return for time spent with my brother?"

Beginning to get more irritated by his comments, she spoke more directly and forcefully. "I wanted nothing, nor did I ever ask for anything. We had the beginning of a special bond. Not lovers, but more than just friends. Why do you think I wanted or tried to profit off your brother's passing?"

"Death! You mean death, Ms. Tolls. So you want me to believe that you had no sights on trying to tap into his vast wealth? *Our* vast wealth? Our family's vast wealth? Is that what you hope for me to fall for?"

Standing and looking down on Alondo, now that she had fully had enough of him, she replied coldly, "Mr. Alondo Regal, I believe I have had enough of your unique company and unintelligent claims of me trying to profit from a heart-wrenching situation, so please excuse me, for I need to return to my office. By the way, an office which pays me a very nice salary, and before that twisted mind of yours gets to spinning, I'm paid well because I'm good at my job. So good that I will take care of the bill today. Goodbye, Alondo."

Shanette paid for their meal and left the waitress a very nice tip, then she walked away from the table and left the restaurant.

Alondo watched her walk out the door then looked at the tip she left. Seeing the waitress coming to collect the money for the bill, he scooped up most of the tip as she approached. Standing in front of her, he said, "The service was not worth this much." He dropped two dollars back down on the table and walked out.

Chapter 7

Let The Mayhem Begin

T'ondra Dove sat in her car singing along with the music on the radio as she drove home. She was puzzled by the request from this Alondo Regal for a meeting. How did he know her and how in the hell could he possibly be able to get Scott to come back to her? As she thought more, her singing went silent, and her mind played out various outcomes. Pulling up to her home, she noticed a car parked out by the curb. Slowing, she looked at the car. It was something expensive and something she had never seen before. Parking in the driveway, T'ondra got out and headed toward the car and person parked out front. By the time she got to the sidewalk, a tall man stood against the side of the vehicle.

Quite attractive, and the suit he wore was impeccable, plus he smelled amazing.

"May I ask who you are and why you are parked in front of my home? You look familiar! You look like that guy who used to advertise for that nightclub."

Then he spoke. His voice was as smooth as silk and honey, with a tone that commanded attention. "Ms. Dove, my name is Regal, Alondo Regal, and as a matter of fact, that guy from the commercials was my brother Anthony. By chance, we have something in common. A troublesome something in common and, with your help, we can both get what we want."

"How do you know what I want? You don't even know me besides my name. According to my assistant, you basically bullied information out of her and into this meeting. So now that you have been met, this meeting… is over. "

Turning to walk away, Regal rose up off the car and caught up with her and spoke again. "You are Ms. Dove, former movie star, former television star, former face of Star Fall sex toys line, formerly with a cook—"

"Master Chef!"

"What the fuck ever! Your recent life has been filled with formers, like Scott Mozell. How would you like to have a current?"

With her curiosity piqued, she took a few steps closer to him. Inhaling his cologne, her body twitched between her legs. Taking a closer, deeper look at Alondo, she saw how handsome he was, and his confidence oozed off him like heat off a fire.

"What do you mean?" she asked, standing close enough to him to feel his response come off his lips.

"How... would you... like to have your muse back? Plainly, I can give you Scott back. With your help, of course."

Excitement filled her face as she thought of Scott Mozell. She never once gave thought to the fact that she had used him for sex and to make her feel good. No thought at all of how he'd caught her cheating on him. No thought of never asking for forgiveness. All she thought of was his encouragement to progress her career and life. "So how do you plan on making this miracle come true? He's with that bitch who works for that little modeling firm downtown." Stepping back, she showed off her body in the skin-tight jeans and open shirt with no bra she was wearing. "If all this couldn't bring him back, why should I believe you can?"

"First of all, from my own experience, The Donovan Modeling Agency was not some little firm. It was rather impressive, but I would never let them catch me saying it, and Mr. Mozell seemed satisfied, not happy. There is a huge difference there."

"Oh, really?"

"You can get a burger and be satisfied," moving close to T'ondra, he ran a hand through the bottom of her hair, "but a delicious, perfectly prepared steak, now that would make you happy!"

Looking deep into Alondo's eyes, searching for a hint of something saying, 'I want you,' T'ondra just stood there. Scanning him from crotch to mouth, she asked again, "How do you plan on accomplishing this?"

"With a little divide and conquer mixed with your unique brand of physical attraction. That is if you have confidence in yourself, Ms. Dove."

Ripping open her shirt and exposing her large full breasts, she stood with her hands on her hips, making sure her arms were keeping the shirt wide open. Now his eyes examined her body like a surgeon looking over a patient. The eyes, though… the eyes glided over every curve of her exposed body, but they still seemed very lifeless and cold. The rise in his crotch area was all the verification she needed to know that the desire to fuck her was still present. If she could arouse this stranger, Scott would be putty in her hands.

"Ms. Dove, if you play your part, I believe we can both get what we want."

"Mr. Regal, let the games begin."

Chapter 8

You or Him?

Scott Mozell sat on the back of his truck sweating and downing a bottle of Gatorade. This remodeling project was extremely difficult due to the constant plan changing by the home owner. Mozell prided himself and his company on providing the best work a person could ask and pay for. Sometimes, but not often, there came a project that just had a hard time coming together. Even rarer than that, was a customer who was too hard to deal with, and this was one of those rarities. Finally done, frustrated workers sent home, with work finally accepted and paid for, Scott longed for a stiff drink as he gathered himself on the tailgate of his work truck.

His phone began ringing, causing him to take a deep breath, thinking to himself, *I hope this isn't Daryl with another job.* Looking at the cell, he didn't recognize the number, but being a businessman, he answered, "Hello, Custom Dreams Remodeling, Scott Mozell."

"Well, how formal. This is Regal, Mr. Mozell. Do you have a moment to spare?"

"As a matter of fact, I have several moments to spare, as my work day is over. What can I do for you?"

"I would like to have a conversation with you. Not by phone if possible."

"Sure. Let me get out of work mode and we can meet up somewhere."

"Well, this is your city. I've already had a luncheon downtown in a rather poor service diner. Maybe you can suggest a better place."

"There is a new place called Cold Mugs, which is a great place for meetings."

"Sounds acceptable; what time shall we say?"

"How about an hour? Since I have your number now, I'll send you the address if that is all right with you."

"I'll be waiting."

***

He clicked his phone off, thinking to himself, *a trashy strip club or horrible bar, I'll guess. Basic trash for a basic man.*

With his head hung down, Alondo walked into Cold Mugs and stopped right in his tracks.

What he had thought would be trash was actually a pretty decent place. No pole, no stage, no sticky floors and no naked women. To that, he was kind of sad, but the environment made up for it. This seemed like a nice, upscale sports bar. There were large screen television sets all around, leather chairs and couches; not premium leather, mind you, but not bad. The waitresses wore black leggings with sport shoes and form fitting jerseys of various sports teams. Seeing Scott sitting in a large chair with an empty chair just like it next to him, he walked over, holding in a smile because he was definitely impressed by this place. When he sat down, a waitress came over and took their order on a digital pad.

"Mr. Mozell, I must saw this place isn't quite the dump I had in mind." Sitting back and crossing his leg, he pointed out all the unique, manly things the place had. Before he knew it, their drinks had arrived. Alondo had ordered a bourbon straight, with one ice cube. The glass wasn't too cold, but chilled enough that the single ice cube wasn't melting. Scott had ordered a beer, and the mug was so cold, vapors came off it.

"Well, Mr. Regal, from what I hear from management, there is still room for improvements, and new ideas are being brought to them daily."

Feeling himself enjoying the atmosphere too much, he decided to get to the reason they were meeting. "Mr. Mozell, let me get right to the point of this gathering. How well do you know Ms. Tolls?"

"What do you mean? She's my lady."

"I mean, do you know her in a way beyond physical? How long have you known her? What is her background like?"

"Slow down, slow down! What are you trying to say about Shanette?"

"No disrespect intended. I was just inquiring about her. Someone who had my brother so twisted around her finger must be an amazing person."

Sitting back and letting the aggression out of his face, Scott took a big swallow of his beer. "All right. She is a special person. She is a friend of mine from way back to high school days. We lost touch for a while, but life changes had our paths cross again."

That was the opening Alondo hoped for. "Lost touch? That must have been the time she fell In love with Anthony. Before he died."

"Well, I guess so, but I can't say they fell in love before he passed."

"He was actually murdered. While they were together. From accounts of the workers at the club, they were a hot item and, possibly, if he was still around, you may not even be in the picture."

***

Stunned by this, Scott had no reply. In his head, he thought about it and knew there was a possibility the man was right.

"What has she told you about him and their relationship?"

"Not a whole lot. It seems to be a difficult subject still for her."

Alondo sipped his drink and raised an eyebrow. "Something is going on there. My words of wisdom would be to find out why it's so hard for her to talk about him if you're the man in her heart."

"You may be right."

Glancing at his watch before continuing, Regal asked Scott if he still had anyone in his heart, like Ms. Tolls. Scott said no, but not convincingly enough.

Alondo commented, "Really? Are you sure?"

Before Scott could answer, someone walked up to the table and caused him to damn near drop his drink.

"Hey, Scott, how you been?"

"Oh, please excuse my rudeness, but I asked someone to meet me here for another meeting. By chance, do you know—"

"T'ondra Dove… yes, I know her."

Standing next to the table, T'ondra had the eyes of every man and a few of the waitresses on her. Wearing an off the shoulder top with stomach showing, thick thighs damn near bursting the seams on the tight skirt she had on, a few noticed her as the TV and movie star she used to be, while others just saw an incredibly sexy woman.

Scott looked up at her and let his eyes explore that body—creamy brown skin, hard nipples poking through her top, a noticeably flatter belly from the personal trainer she used while promoting the sex toys on late night infomercials. The jeans she wore curved around and hugged her candy area. Scott could see no panties were on, or he figured no panties were on, because that was the kind of woman she was.

"Hey, Scott, how have you been? You're looking good. Can an old friend have a hug for old times' sake?"

Scott wanted to stand and give her that hug, but certain situations had arisen, making it kind of… hard… for him to do so.

Alondo sat back and smiled. By Scott not getting up, he knew there must be something still inside that cared for or at least liked T'ondra.

While his eyes lusted for Dove and his penis jumped at the remembrance of the sex they'd had, his mind kicked in, bringing back images of her and that guy co-star having real sex in front of the studio crew then how she'd ignored him, for more dick in her trailer.

"I asked Ms. Dove to come by because my time is short and valuable. So please excuse me while I go relieve myself from my drink. Mr. Mozell, I believe you have given me all the information I need. Remember what we discussed about Ms. Tolls. Ask her! Ms. Dove, give me just a few moments."

T'ondra leaned down and put her hands on the table in front of Scott and smiled. When she did, her loose shirt drooped down, showing anyone who could see her very large breasts swinging.

Scott's eyes locked onto her chest looking like two milk chocolate globes with Hershey Kiss nipples. His mouth started to water, thinking of the last time his lips and tongue were massaging them.

Now his penis was getting so hard that it was causing his zipper to open up.

"Do you miss me, Scott?"

Sitting back in his chair and sipping a beer, he answered, "Not at all!"

T'ondra reached over and caressed the bulge in his pants. "I think you do, or at least a… big… part of you does."

He grabbed her hand to push it away, but she was able to slide her hand down and open his pants more. With her free hand, she pulled up a chair and sat next to him. The sounds of fans cheering and games on every screen had everyone's attention, so no one paid attention to Dove sitting next to Mozell with her hand on his cock. Slowly, she stroked it up and down, whispering in his ear, "Bet your little business bitch doesn't stroke you like this and her throat isn't as deep as mine."

He went to push her back away from him by moving her legs, but she opened them. Because she was wearing a short skirt, when he pushed, his hand went straight to her honey pot. At least two of his fingers went inside.

Scott's heart damn near stopped, feeling the wetness of that pool she called a pussy. Still stroking him, she closed her thighs, trapping his fingers inside, and began to move her hips around and around.

"Wonder if we could get away with more? How about I sit on your lap until Alondo is ready to go?"

Now, sweat was coming down his face and it wasn't from the hot wings he'd had. Saving the day and stopping a major mistake, Alondo appeared from the restroom and stepped up to the table. Looking at the waitress who'd served them, he left the exact amount for his meal and a dollar tip. "Mr. Mozell," then he nodded toward him, "Ms. Dove, let's proceed." Then he turned and walked away.

T'ondra released Scott from her thigh death grip and placed his sticky fingers in her mouth, licking herself off them. "Damn, I taste good. See, if I sat on your lap, I could have sucked it off something else. When you get tired of that lazy, boring sex, you can always come ride this pussy-coaster." Then she walked out as well.

Scott wiped the sweat from his head and called the waitress over. He paid his bill, looked at Alondo's tip, and handed her twenty dollars. Then he got up and quickly made his way out. In his vehicle, he checked his watch. Shanette was still at work, and this erection needed attention. The more he thought of it, Shanette wouldn't be down to throw down like he wanted to now, so it was time to go home and put the beast in his pants down himself. '*Fucking T'ondra,*' he thought to himself as he drove off.

Chapter 9

Be Honest

Another day downtown in the city brought multiple people in suits, rushing up and down the blocks on cell phones, oblivious to each other passing by unless someone cut off their path. Among the crowd, walked two women, laughing and enjoying the midday weather, too busy with each other to care about the surrounding public. Before the women could reach their destination, a sub sandwich shop that just recently opened, a man called out to them.

"Shanette! Dom! Hold up. Slow down."

"Oh, hey, hun."

"Hey, Chubbs, what's good with you?"

"Not a thing, Dom. What's good?"

"It's all good, Chubbs, but I can't find a good enough man to prove it to."

Shanette gently pushed Dominece's shoulder as she laughed. "Okay. You gonna find a man to put it on you."

"I don't want it put on me. I need it put in me. It's been way too long. I may have to start giving my toy those blue pills now, just to keep up."

Scott dropped his head and Shanette rolled her eyes. Dominece burst out in laughter, almost falling back into a woman passing by.

Scott then took Shanette's hand and asked her a question quietly. "I know y'all are on the way to lunch, but can I ask you a kind of important question real quick?"

"Sure, Scott, what's up?"

"Here? In front of Dom? Can we do this in private?"

"Is it something that serious?"

Seeing the concern growing on Shanette's face, he told her it wasn't that major of a deal and here would be fine. "Can I ask you about that guy Regal?"

"Who, Alondo? I don't know much about him except he is kind of an arrogant ass."

"No, not Alondo. His brother Anthony. "

The mention of Anthony's name put a blank expression on Shanette's face and surprise on Dominece's. Dom said, "Maybe I should leave you two in private."

Hearing Dom say that let Scott know there had to be more feeling there than he had been told. Why would she hide this from him? True, the guy was before him and actually had nothing to do with him, but if she was still holding on to something, he should know about it.

"What about Anthony, Scott? I told you all about him," Shanette said.

"You told me about him, but not all about him. Did you love him?"

"Why are you asking me this now? *We* are together now."

"Yes, we are. Partly."

"Partly! What the fuck does that mean?"

"I don't think you have been completely honest with me. If you had love for him while you were together, it's one thing, but if you are still in love with him, it's a whole other issue."

***

Dominece broke into the conversation and moved closer to her friend, sensing she may go off and this may escalate into an unnecessary argument. "What difference does it make, Scott? You are the man in her life now…"

Just then, an odd-colored limo rode by, catching Dominece's eye. She thought to herself that the limo looked familiar. Then she put her attentions back on her friends. "Anthony is the past. You're the present. Isn't that good enough, Chubbs?"

"It would be, Dom, if her heart was completely into us, but if a part of it still belongs to him, how can we have a true and deep relationship?"

Thinking for a quick second, Dom agreed with Scott's statement by nodding toward him. She then looked at Shanette and asked her what she'd told him about Anthony.

"I told him I did care for him—"

"Care! Bitch, even I know... Hell, we all knew you two were in love. Being around y'all, anyone could see it."

Speechless, Shanette looked at Dom with disbelief and aggression. Then sadness overtook her face, knowing Dominece had just told the truth about her. Her eyes diverted to Scott, seeing the sadness in his face.

"So, you still have love for him and have been withholding it from me?"

"Scott, where is all this coming from?"

"Alondo told me."

"Alondo? How in the hell does he know—"

Scott interrupted her, taking a step backwards. "Doesn't matter how he knew. He didn't even live here, and he knew. So what does that say?"

Dominece said, "Damn! He is an asshole," quietly behind Shanette.

"Can we talk about this, Scott? Please?" She reached out to put her hands on his chest, but he grabbed her hands before she could.

"Not right now. I've heard all I need to hear right now."

As Scott walked to his truck and drove away, Dominece hugged her friend, trying to comfort her with an embrace and kind words of reassurance. Then the limo that had caught her eye when it had driven by was parked on the curb, several feet down. They women walked toward it, going back to the Donovan Agency, when the door opened and a man stepped out.

Anger overflowed from Shanette as she saw who stepped from the car. "Alondo, you piece of shit! How dare you start crap between me and Scott."

The man walked closer, with the sun at his back. Shanette moved quickly to confront him and release all her anger on him. Dominece followed closely behind.

"Why would you do that to me and my relationship? What did I ever do to you, Alondo? I never asked for nothing from your brother and I sure as fuck don't want anything from you! And how in the hell did you grow… a… full… beard?"

Squinting her eyes through the sun to look into his eyes, she noticed a gleam Alondo usually didn't have. Only one person had that gleam.

"Anthony?"

"How are you, my dear?"

Chapter 10

Common Agenda

Alondo followed T'ondra back to her home per her request, to discuss how the set up with Scott had gone. He'd actually had his fill of lesser people to last a couple of lifetimes by now. Across the ocean, he was accustomed to finer living, the best foods, finest of wines, and the money to attract women. Anything he wanted, but he thought to himself that some of the women here in the States were most pleasing. Watching Ms. Dove as she walked confirmed this thought.

***

Looking back over her shoulder, she could see Alondo's eyes scanning her body. T'ondra had also examined him, considering if his dick could be a quick option or not. The size seemed good enough through his suit pants, but size without ability to use it was worthless.

Once inside, she offered him a drink. Alondo glanced over her liquor options and sighed. "Your best cognac, that is if you have any cognac."

"Hennessy or Martel?"

"If that's the best you have, I'll take whichever one you've had the longest." He looked at the couch before sitting down, then frowned. Adjusting his suit coat, he just walked the room, looking around. "So, Ms. Dove. This is what being a movie and television star affords you?"

"I decided not to waste money on a big mansion. Just in case my career took a down turn."

"Well, your bank account must be overflowing."

If eyes could talk, they'd just called him an asshole, but she knew getting Scott back in her life would be a tremendous confidence booster. So dealing with this arrogant bastard was necessary. "Here's your drink, Alondo."

Without a thank you or even a nod to simulate a thank you, he looked the glass over and took a small swallow of the alcohol before setting it down on the nearest table. "How do you think it went with Mozell? Hopefully you played your part well enough."

Very offended that Alondo questioned her sex appeal, she went over and snatched the glass up off the table and spilled the rest of the drink on her clothes. Now even more aggravated, she looked at him as he continued to judge her and her home. Then a smirk came across her face. He had doubts about her ability. Oh, really, well, he would see it firsthand. Shit, she was already horny from using Scott's fingers.

"If you don't mind, I need a minute to change shirts. Like you, my time is valuable too."

"If you say so. Please make it quick so we can discuss our next move."

T'ondra left the room for a few minutes then reappeared out of the hallway with what was basically nothing on. She stood there wearing thin leather straps that only covered her nipples and met between her legs with another thin strap that covered just the split between her legs. T'ondra had always had an eye catching body, even in her early career in movies. After she linked her name to sex toys, she tightened up the sex appeal. Her chest was still large and firm, waist not too small, but no body hang over, either. Those thick thighs were so inviting, anyone would want to settle down between them.

Alondo felt electricity shoot up and through his penis, but his face was a stone, as ever. When she walked over and stood with her legs gapped in front of him, he could feel the muscles in his legs twitching.

"This is one of the items I used to sell. What do you think?" she asked while rubbing her breasts and nipples under the straps.

"You have quite the body, Ms. Dove. Very different than the slim model type overseas."

She ran her hands over her plump brown ass and unbuckled the straps, letting the leather garment fall to her feet. "That feels so much sexier to me. The outfit is good for an appetizer, but the full meal is what's in it."

Trying not to let his lust take control, he put his hands in his pockets and held that muscle that brings and receives pleasure, squeezing it. "Ms. Dove, how is this going to accomplish our goals? We need—"

T'ondra put two of her fingers inside herself while twirling them until they were wet and slightly creamy. Then she put them up to Alondo's lips, stopping him from talking. "Shhh! I'll show you how I'm going to accomplish my goal." Then using her other hand, she unzipped his pants. The bulge gave away the fact he was indeed aroused but may have needed her help releasing that erection. His penis grew as the air of the room hit it. With bare cock in hand, she felt the warmth of his mouth taking in her wet fingers, sipping them clean and dry.

The insatiable yearning and unquenchable nature of Dove took over. True, she wanted Scott back in her life, but having a well-built, handsome man's dick in her face was far too tempting. Plus, the fact that he doubted her ability gave her that extra drive to prove her point. Using her tongue as a guide, she slid her mouth around the pulsating penis. Be it less than a mouthful, she still tried to suck the feeling out of it.

***

Never had he had a woman delight herself so with his cock. Feeling he was losing control over the situation, he grabbed the back of her head and forcefully thrust himself into her throat. He wasn't large or thick, but being shoved down her mouth became very unpleasant quickly.

She tried to pull away, but he had a strong grip on her head. T'ondra pushed on his legs, trying to back him off her.

"You like choking on this dick, don't you?"

T'ondra coughed and choked, trying to speak, but with every word she tried to say, he pushed harder. Having the upper hand again, Alondo picked her up and pushed her over the arm of a couch. Now bent over with that ass in the air, he dropped his pants and kicked her legs open. "Let's see how you like this, you little bitch."

T'ondra didn't mind a guy being vocal with her and also was up for some physical sex, but this guy was being too forceful. Shit! If she hadn't started it off by sucking on his dick, this would be considered rape. "Take it easy, man! I'm giving you the pussy."

"You're not giving me shit! I'm taking this hot pussy and you love it." Then he took a hand full of her hair, twisted it and pulled hard. As he did so, he let his iron hard muscle dive inside Dove, but it didn't enter her slowly drying pussy. It was thrust into her clenched tight asshole. She yelled out in pain, but to his ears, it sounded like sweet singing.

"Stop! Stop, motherfucker, you're in my ass. This hurts. Stop!"

Alondo kept pounding harder and faster until he pulled out and exploded on her back. Crawling over the arm onto the couch, she lay there holding her butt in pain. Lucky for her, he wasn't a marathon man, but a short distance sex man.

"I guess that twat will do. That is if he is a lesser man than I am, you might be able to work him. Well, you had him before so I guess it's good enough for him."

"You son of a bitch, I was going to give you a shot of this shit between my legs. You damn near pulled my hair out and my ass had better not be bleeding. I didn't give you permission to fuck my ass."

Looking around and seeing a shirt of hers that was lying in a chair, he wiped his dick off and tossed it at her, then pulled his pants up. "I planted the seed of distrust in Mr. Mozell's mind, so I need you and that subpar ass to grow that doubt. The clock is ticking, Ms. Dove. Hurry!"

"Don't worry about my end. And what's the hurry? Why do you need them apart so fast?"

"That is my business, and I suggest you mind your own and let me tend to that fortune snatching whore."

T'ondra's eyes widened as she realized why he was after her so bad. His dead brother must have left her money and he felt like it should be his. The dirty, tricky bastard.

As Alondo opened the door, he looked over his shoulder. "Tick tock, Ms. Dove. You'll regret it dearly if time runs out." Then he let the door slam behind himself.

Chapter 11

How?

Dominece stared at the man standing in front of her and Shanette. She was told of Anthony's twin brother being in town and not being very nice. Shit! Who was she kidding, this guy Alondo was an ass. Although she hadn't had the chance of meeting him and setting his punk ass straight, this guy had a very familiar vibe. It couldn't be, though. Anthony was dead. She was at his funeral and saw his coffin go in the ground. That dog ass bastard Pit had caused his death, but this dude here... something about this dude!

Shanette was speechless but walked toward him slowly and put her hands up to the man's face.

Rubbing his beard and looking his face all over, Shanette was trying to recognize a feature. There was no way Alondo could have grown hair on his face that fast, and by the feel of the beard, it was real. Anthony was dead and buried, but something... Then she looked into his eyes and saw a spark, glow, a gleam. She held her hand against his face and searched for words. "Anthony! How are you?" Then she stumbled backwards.

Dominece grabbed her waist from behind as the man reached out to hold her up by the arms.

"Shanette, are you okay?"

"What the hell do you think? She just saw a ghost. No, she's not all right. Matter of fact, I'm not either."

"Anthony, how?"

"My dear, let us help you. Once you regain your composure, I'll tell you everything. The both of you."

***

Back in Shanette's office at The Donovan Agency, Anthony leaned up against the desk with his arms folded and looked at everyone, seeing shock, confusion and slight anger on Dominece's face. Dom would be the mad one. In the room, sat Shanette and Dom, of course, along with Vikki Donovan, Jack Arms and Toni Voss, the whole managing force of the agency.

Jack Arms, Co-V.P. looked around the office then stood up and asked, "How do we know this isn't Alondo somehow? Anthony was—"

"A kind man," Toni supplied.

"A very caring man," Vikki said as she looked at Shanette.

"A very dead man!" Shanette stood up and gestured a quiet motion with her hand. "Explain! If you can."

Letting out a breath, he began, "That night after I was hit by that Pit guy, Anita's ex guy, I did die. Or so to speak. I coded on the operating table and was pronounced dead that night. The sheet was thrown over me. According to the doctors, on the way to the basement morgue, an accident happened which turned out to be a stroke of luck.

Dominece sat forward and asked, "How does an accident become luck? What the fuck happened? You get struck by lightning?"

"In a way, yes. The person who was taking my body down was careless and pushed my gurney into a stand holding a faulty defibrillator. The paddles had fallen onto my gurney when he tried to push the stand back against the wall. In doing so, he turned on the defibrillator. Supposedly, the machine was stuck on full charge when on. The discharge sent a jolt through the paddles to the metal, then to me and my heart, giving me a super jump start, in a way."

"But you were dead, right?" Jack asked as he stood and walked the room.

"Yes, for over...over...over. Yes, for overrrr. Please forgive me."

Shanette walked over and held his hand.

"For over ten minutes. The doctors said that going that long with no oxygen going to my brain, I would have issues, such as speech, motor skills and memory blanks."

Then everyone else came over to him. His story sounded insane and impossible, but he explained it so convincingly, they believed in the impossible. Toni and Vikki hugged him. Even Dom believed him, asking if he would be able to recover and be his old self after some time.

"I'm afraid not, my dear. My condition is permanent and could worsen over time." Tears formed in his eyes as he looked up, trying to keep them there in his eyes.

"But who was buried at your funeral?" Ms. Donovan asked as she gave him a skeptical look.

"That was another poor soul who died in the same hospital. Upon my coming back to life, they asked who they should call to come and get me. Shanette would've been the one called, but I couldn't get her name out, and I still don't remember her number. Fortunately, my lawyer had come to verify my demise. I was released into his care."

"Why didn't he call me?"

"He has no knowledge of you, dear. Mr. Bulksail is an estate attorney. My family made a lot of money in real estate. They used to own huge areas of property in different states which were sold at twenty times the original purchase price then that was invested and doubled. On their passing, my brother and I inherited that fortune. Alondo took his share as soon as the dirt settled on my mother's grave. Father had passed years earlier."

"Really?"

"Yes. 'Do' moved to Europe, blew through his money and has been in hiding from collectors for years."

"Do?"

"Alondo. That is what I used to call him when we were kids. I haven't spoken to him since he went to Europe."

"What happened to your share?"

"It's still in the bank. I got a job and made my own way and own a small fortune through good business deals. Mr. Bulksail thought it would be a good idea to fake my burial, to bring my greedy brother out of hiding because, with my passing, my share goes to him."

Shanette nodded her head. "No wonder he has been pestering me. He must think you left me your money in a will, after hearing we must have been together."

Anthony continued to talk to everyone about his brother and his past treachery. Soon, the executives went back to work while Shanette and

Dominece walked Anthony out to his limo. Outside, Shanette held Anthony tightly and looked into his eyes. She told him how she'd missed him and how unbelievable all that had happened to him and how he was back seemed. She kissed him on the cheek, and he kissed her forehead.

As he entered the car, a man was standing closely behind them. The car pulled away the very moment Shanette and Dom turned to see the man.

"Scott!"

"Chubbs! Oh shit."

Chapter 12

Mistakes

Scott rode home, mixed emotions warring inside himself—the hurt of Shanette not being honest about her feelings against the seemingly ease of disregarding the fact he was currently the so called man in her life. The more he thought, the faster he drove. He only followed the direction of the car, which had no destination, but to get as far away from downtown as possible. His cell rang again and he glanced at it. Shanette was calling again. He gripped the steering wheel tighter and pushed the gas pedal harder. There was a busy intersection coming up soon, and Scott simply saw the straight away of the road. Once again, the phone rang. This time, it snapped him back to sanity, causing him to slow and stop at a red light, avoiding a major catastrophe. When he looked this time, it was Dominece. He thought about not answering her call, either, but thought better of it. Ignoring Shanette was one thing, but Dom was a whole other problem. One he truly didn't want. You would rather have a rabid grizzly bear mad at you than her.

Pulling over in front of a home in one of the better neighborhoods, he answered his phone. "Yes, Dom."

"Why didn't you answer when Shanette called you? You need to get your ass back down here now and talk this shit out."

"Right now, Dom, I have nothing to talk to her about."

"The fuck you don't. You know how she feels about you."

"Do I?" Out of the corner of his eye, he saw someone coming down the drive of the house he was in front of.

"Yes, you do, Chubbs. She has always cared for you—"

"Cared for me. That's it. Cared! She was… is in love with that dead guy who, all of a sudden, seems to be very alive now."

"We just found out ourselves. The story about it is insanely crazy, but it's believable when you hear it. Come on back, so she can explain it to you herself."

As Scott sat and contemplated going back, the figure in the driveway had now come down to his car and knocked on his window. "Dom, I have to go." Then he hung up.

"Hey, Scott. I see thoughts of this platinum puss has brought you back to my place."

Scott looked around and saw he had stopped in front of T'ondra Dove's home. How and why in the hell did he stop here? He didn't mean to come here. Did he? No, hell no. He got out and slammed the car door, not in anger toward T'ondra, but from anger in general. The anger he used to feel about T' had long passed due to having his true dream in his life, Shanette, or so he thought. He loved her, but did she have the same kind of love for him?

"T'ondra, I did not plan to come here, believe me. I have a lot on my mind right now and I just happened to stop to collect myself here. If I knew where I was, I would not have stopped."

"Well, that's harsh. We were friends once upon a time—"

"Yes, we were at one time."

Dove asked, "What's really going on with you? Can I help?"

He gave her a dry thank you but told her no, that he had to straighten this out himself. She invited him in to talk, and he declined. He knew she couldn't be trusted not to tempt him somehow, sexually, and being hurt by Shanette wouldn't help. Emotions would be all over the place and the possibility of making a mistake and regretting it was high.

Ms. Dove tried her hardest to get Scott to come in so she could use her body to coerce him to lie with her again. She even went as far as dropping her cell phone and bending over to pick it up, but not like a normal person would. She bent over at the waist in paper thin white leggings, showing her plump juicy peach to Scott, the world and anyone who could or wanted to see.

Past sexual experiences the two shared flooded his mind, the time in the window, all the times in the pool. Even that time they got caught in the park by a couple jogging by when she was giving him oral sex on a picnic table. Instead of stopping, she became more animated with it, to be noticed. The couple had stopped to watch, not believing what they were seeing. Scott had never come so hard. Plus, T'ondra never took her mouth off him, swallowing all he was giving.

Just as something began to rise in his pants, thoughts of Shanette came to mind—her smile, her touch, the way he felt just having her around. He loved her, truly loved her. She could fulfill everything in his wildest dreams. T'ondra was just a lust filled fantasy and could be nothing more.

He went over to T'ondra and put his hand on the side of her face. "T', I know what you are trying to do, and it's not going to work. You want me back. I'm not actually sure for what reason, but you do want me back. You feel something for me, but it's not love. That I do know."

She placed her hand over his and looked into his eyes. She could see there was care in his eyes by the way he looked at her. It was a look she had never really given him. She didn't love him, never did. She loved the way he made her feel and the way he made her feel about herself. "Scott, I—"

"T'. I know; you don't have to say it. You only want me back because I gave you everything you were missing in your life. Everything but love. You're not ready to love yet and may not be able to love, ever. We can be friends, and that's it. What we had in the past is just that, it's in the past."

T'ondra was stunned by Scott's response because it hit home. No matter what sexual advance she tried on him, nothing was going to work. Honestly, if he was with her again, there was no way she would want another bitch trying to serve him some side ass, unless she set it up and was joining in. She wanted that dedication from a man... someday.

Ms. Dove moved from the front of Scott's car back to the driveway. For the first time, she felt uncomfortable in what she was wearing. She crossed her arms and dropped her head. "Scott, I, uh… I, uh…" She looked up at him and started to cry.

He came over to her and grabbed her by the arms. "What's wrong?"

"Scott, I want to say I'm sorry. Sorry for basically being a bitch to you, acting like a whore in front of you, and taking advantage of your friendship."

Shocked by what he'd just heard, Scott damn near fell over. First, he thought this might be another ploy from her to get him to drop his emotional guard, but those tears were too real, and the shaky, soft sound in her voice was something he had never heard from her before.

"T', I… that's all I ever wanted from you. I forgave you for all that long ago, but to hear you say you're sorry and mean it, that is amazing." He walked over and hugged her. He felt an exhale as she sunk deep into his arms and cried even more.

When he finally let go and she stopped crying, she looked at him and asked, "Can we possibly be friends again?"

He replied, "As long as you can keep it friend based, I would be proud to have Ms. T'ondra Dove as my friend."

She kissed him on the cheek and went back up the driveway with a normal walk. No switch, no booty bouncing, just a regular walk away. Scott smiled as she did so then got back in his car to drive home and think about how he was going to handle the situation with Shanette.

Chapter 13

Regals

Shanette sat on the edge of her couch, staring at a half empty bottle of wine on the table while holding another full glass. Dominece, on the hand, was drinking whiskey straight from the bottle.

"Girl, it wasn't my guy who reappeared from the grave, but I feel your pain, bitch. What the hell are you going to do?"

Shanette took another big sip of wine and made a move to put it down but came inches away from the table and swallowed another gulp. "What am I going to do about Anthony still being alive? Shit, I don't know."

"Bitch! That and Chubbs. You know that man adores you and Anthony was definitely feeling you before, you know, he resurrected."

"I have no idea. I know Scott has feelings for me—"

"Feelings? That man loves you and has since college. Shit, since high school. You never seemed to get to that point with Anthony."

Standing up, walking to the kitchen and coming back with some chips, Shanette told her friend that she and Anthony never had a chance to evolve into anything.

Then Dom asked her if she had told Scott about her incomplete feelings toward Regal.

Shanette had a blank look on her face. "I guess I haven't. Mainly, because I don't know how

I feel. Scott has been so good to me and I guess he deserves to know, either way."

Just then her phone buzzed with a text message: *This is Sindel Free, personal assistant to Anthony Regal. He asked me to reach out to you and ask if it's possible for him to come by to pay a visit.* She showed Dom the text.

"Why the hell is he having an assistant text you? I'm damn sure he knows your address because he picked you up here for a date."

"That's true."

"Are you sure that was from Anthony?"

"Yes. I still have his number in my phone, but why couldn't he call me himself?"

***

After some time arguing with himself, he got out of his car in front of Shanette's place when a large black car pulled up next to him. A guy got out and opened the door, letting a tall man with a scruffy beard out.

The two men looked at each other, and Scott asked, "Alondo, what are you doing here?"

"Excuse me? Oh, you must know my brother."

The serious look on Scott's face turned into a frown. "That would make you Anthony, Anthony Regal. The dead has arisen, man."

"I suppose that is an accurate description, albeit rude. Who might you be, sir, since I am at a loss since losing time off my life?"

"My name is Scott Mozell."

"Are you a friend of my brother's?"

"Not exactly. I met your brother once and have heard some not so good things about him from Shanette."

"Oh, you are a friend of Shanette's."

"Friends? You can say that—" Right at that moment, another car pulled up and a well-dressed man got out and looked at the two men with a scowl for one, then shock at the other.

"What in the complete fuck? Why are you alive?"

"Hello, Londo. It doesn't seem like you are too happy to see me. And why am I alive? Is that any kind of way to greet your brother?"

"You're supposed to be dead! They told me you were dead. Why aren't you dead, Tony?" Alondo yelled as he walked closer to his brother and bumped Scott as he passed by.

The two brothers stood face to face. Scott stepped back from them and looked from one to the other. Besides the clothes on Alondo and the beard on Anthony, the two were identical. Not wanting to be involved in a family argument, he left the parking area and went up to Shanette's door.

***

The doorbell rang, and Shanette looked at her friend then the clock. "Well, I guess we're going to find out what's going on." She got up and opened the door. Surprised by the face looking back at her, she asked, "Scott, what are you doing here?"

Irritation, hurt and anger mixed for a voice coming out of Scott that Shanette had never heard. "Do I need a reason to come see you, or am I not the person you were expecting or wanting to see?"

"No, no, that's not it. You know I always want to see you, dear."

"Is that so? Hey, Dom. What's up, girl?"

"Hey, Chubbs. What going down, sucka?" Then she erupted in laughter. "Come give me a hug."

Shanette closed the door after he came inside. "What's wrong, Scott? Are you mad at me?"

Ignoring her, he talked to Dominece. "Going down, sucka? You bring out your inner soul sister?" Then he hugged her. With his arm still around Dominece, he said, "Shanette, we need to talk."

Dom told them she would go, so they could straighten things out, but Scott told her to stay. She had always been like a sister to him and that made her family, so he insisted she be there.

***

Outside, the brothers continued to stare at each other until Anthony broke the silence. "How are you doing, Londo? I see your time overseas wasn't all bad."

"What the fuck you know about my overseas time? As you can see, my ventures were very profitable."

"Was that before or after your prison stay?"

The last of his cool demeanor left Alondo's voice. "How did you know about that? Besides, it's none of your damn business. Where were you when I was locked up? Where were you when I needed you?"

Anthony stepped up to his brother's chest and looked him square in the eyes. "Where was I?

Where were you when Uncle Lawrence was dying?"

"Lawrence! Why the fuck would I want or need to be there while he was dying?"

"Because after our parents died, Uncle Lawrence took care of us like his own. He loved us; he loved you! Always, 'have you heard from Londo?' 'Have you spoken to Londo?' 'Find him and make sure he has money.' That man was everything to us when we needed him."

"Whatever. I took care of myself."

Slapping his brother's chest, Anthony answered, "And what a marvelous job you have done with that. Look, I'm not here to argue with you, Londo. You are my brother and I love you. Always have and always will. Now, I know about the money problems you have over there, and I want to help. Our accountant told me you're a couple hundred thousand in the red with some of your partners and they're looking for you. Let me help."

Trying to regain his normal alpha male demeanor, Alondo turned his back to Anthony and said, "There you go, always having to be the best, the savior, the fucking best, bigger man! You were always the favorite. With our parents, Uncle Lawrence, and just about anyone we came in contact with."

"Londo, we were treated the same. You treated all of us like we were nothing or less than you. Ever since we were young, you did this shit. You caused all your own problems, Londo, and all we did was try to help you fix them."

"You want to fix my problems now? Crawl back in the grave and stay there." He got back in his car, slammed the door and sped away.

Chapter 14

Who's the Better Man?

As Scott came outside after his conversation with Shanette, he ran into Anthony again. He noticed Anthony wasn't the same as when he had first run into him, and he wondered what happened between him and his brother. *Not my concern*, he thought.

Anthony was just standing in the parking lot, looking around like he was lost. The man just didn't seem right and Scott's good nature wouldn't let him feel any kind of anger right now.

"Excuse me, Anthony, is everything all right?"

"Yeah, yeah." Then he paused and looked at Scott. "You're Shanette's friend, right?"

Puzzled, he answered, "Yes, I'm Scott. We met few minutes ago, right before your talk with your brother."

"Scott… I believe you to be a good and honest man. I don't know you, but I can feel that about you."

"Thank you. I try my best to live up to a high standard."

"Since you are a friend of Shanette's, that makes you a trustworthy friend. Most of her friends are, except for that female friend she used to have who was the cause of all my misery. Her name escapes me now—"

"Anita Watts? They were friends, or close associates, since college, until one of her boy toys tried to kill her and ended up killing you. Or so everyone thought."

"Yes. That's her name. Since she was a friend of Shanette's, I felt obligated to help her."

"Okay, time to address the pink elephant in the room. How are you alive? Did you fake your death?"

Once again, Anthony went over what he was told happened, even about the void between him and his brother. Scott asked him why it took so long after the funeral for him to contact anyone.

"Well, that was the decision of my accountant. He knew of my brother's money woes and figured that once he heard of my death, he would return for my share of the family money and any of my private funds he could get. Once here, he would be turned over to international police, but I wanted to try to help. Always trying to save."

Scott looked at him and immediately felt differently about the man. He had him figured out all wrong. On the surface and at his core, this was a good dude and someone he would probably have hung out with.

"One other thing. I'm not right mentally."

"What do you mean, Anthony, you crazy now or something?"

"No, no, nothing like that. Since my return from death, I've been having memory blanks. At times, it takes some time for things to come back to me. Other things don't come unless I get help, like you did with Ms. Watts and my manager finding Shanette's number for me in my own damn phone. There are parts of my memory and some motor function that are just gone forever. I'm basically useless to anyone. Even though I have strong feelings for Shanette, I would not want to burden her with my declining condition."

"I am so sorry for you, my man. I wish there was some way I could help you."

"As I said before, a good man." Then he smiled at Scott. "She needs a man like you, a constant stable fixture. I'm a turbulent world."

The two men shook hands and separated. After Scott pulled away, Anthony looked around and scratched his head. Then he got in his car, told the navigation system to make a route to Chocolate Silk and pulled away, completely forgetting he was there to see Shanette.

Chapter 15

Pain of Love

Alondo paced back and forth in his hotel room with rage burning in his gut and fire in his eyes. He caught a glimpse of himself in a mirror on the wall. Not seeing himself, but Anthony, he punched through the mirror and the wall behind it. He wondered why he didn't cry when he got the news his brother was dead. He didn't feel any remorse. Nothing! Now that the money being held wasn't going to be his, all he felt, all he wanted, was for Anthony to be out of the way. He wasn't even a brother to him now. He was just a man named Anthony who had his money.

His phone rang, but he only noticed it after several rings. That whore T'ondra Dove. He didn't need her anymore, but maybe he could use her to get Anthony out of the way now, instead of that Mozell bastard and Tolls bitch.

"Dove, I need you to—"

"Alondo, I can't do it."

"Do what?"

"Hurt Scott. I no longer want... I only want the best for him 'cause he deserves it. He deserves better than me, and if it's Shanette, so be it. I'd rather have him as a true friend than a bitter partner."

"You fucking useless slut. All you motherfuckers are completely useless. I'll take care of all of them my damn self."

"Fuck you, Alondo! Wait, take care of all of whom?"

"Stay out of my way, bitch. You had your chance, and you had the sex of your life with me. Now run along and go back to being the washed up hack of an actress you are." Then he hung up. He went into the bedroom, pulling a small case from under the bed. He opened it, checked the contents, then hurried out the door, letting it slam behind him.

***

T'ondra stood in the doorway of her home, calling Scott to warn him that Alondo had flipped out. No answer. She grabbed her keys, deciding to go over to Shanette's house herself and warn her. Good thing she'd stalked and followed Scott those few times. She knew exactly where she lived and wanted to warn her... for Scott's sake.

***

Dominece hugged her friend before starting to leave. As she opened the door, her face turned ghostly white. "Oh my God!"

Shanette looked around her friend to see who had shocked her so. "Oh, shit. You're here. Come in."

"Why are you here? What the hell! Someone had better tell me something, dammit, before the neighbors call the police on me!"

"I see nothing has changed with you, Dom."

"Come on in, Anita, and sit down. You okay, need any help?"

She walked past, and Dominece looked down to see Anita was walking with a cane. Her first thought was to knock that bitch out again like she had at the funeral, but she needed to know why she was here and why Shanette was being so nice to her. This trick was the reason Anthony had died in the first place. "Shanette! Bitch! You'd better explain this shit before this crippled bitch gets knocked out again!"

Shanette sat them down and began to explain why Anita was there and what had happened to her. During the talk, she got two texts—one from Scott and the other from Anthony. She told both of them to come back over so things could be cleared up between all of them.

A short while later, Anita and Dominece left. Dom was no longer wanting to knock Anita out, and she even gave her a genuine hug as they left. Before she could close the door, Anthony pulled up and got out. As he walked across the lot, Scott pulled in as well.

"Hello, Scott, fancy meeting you here...
again." Then he laughed as they shook hands.
Another car was pulling in as the two men
continued walking together. A man got out and ran
to them, punching one of them. Anthony fell to the
ground, looking up to see Alondo standing over him
with a balled fist.

"You die today, Anthony, and I'm going to
make sure you stay dead this time." He reached in
his waistband and was dazed by a hard right hand
from Scott. Another car came rushing by and
parked farther down the lot. Shanette left her
doorway, running, intending to break up the fight.
Scott continued to tussle with Alondo as Anthony
got up and joined in the brawl. Falling back against
the car, Alondo pulled a gun from his waist and

pointed it at Anthony, causing him to freeze in his tracks.

"Londo, don't do this. We're brothers."

"We were never brothers!"

Before he could shoot, Shanette stood in front of Anthony, begging for him not to shoot. Then Scott tried to move her out of the way.

"Doesn't matter who catches the first bullet. I got one for all of y'all. Then he aimed at Shanette and pulled the trigger. From the side, another person ran in and took the bullet.

A cane came in then and bashed Alondo in the face, causing him to lower the gun.

Several sets of eyes looked at the person on the ground bleeding. Scott knelt down, screaming, "No!"

Anthony rushed at his brother to keep him from shooting anyone else. Dominece and Anita come up behind Scott in a panic. It was Dom swinging Anita's cane that had caused Alondo to lower the gun.

"Someone call 911. Please call 911 now!"

The two ladies pulled their friend back. "Shanette, back up before that fool shoots you like he did Scott's old girl."

Scott sat on the ground holding T'ondra. "You're not that bad. Hold on. You're only hit in the side, just be still. Why did you do that?"

"I couldn't let you get shot. I knew what he was coming to do and you wouldn't answer your phone. So I came to warn your girlfriend."

The moment was broken by three more shots. Everyone looked over at the two brothers.

Anthony's eyes widened as he began to shake. Alondo still had the look of pure hate in his eyes as he peered into Anthony's while they teared up. Then he fell into his brother's arms.

"I am so sorry, Londo. I couldn't let you hurt any more of these good people. Whatever I did to you or didn't do for you, please forgive me. No matter what, you are my brother and I love you. I love you to death, brother." Then he held him in his arms until that last breath of hate left Alondo's lungs.

Epilogue

Scott and Shanette left the hospital after checking on T'ondra.

Anthony was at the police station with his accountant, giving a statement about Alondo. Anita and Dominece were also there, as witnesses. It had hurt him to his heart to kill his only brother, but his friends were his new and true family. Another crazy situation was when Anthony told T'ondra he was a big fan of hers and that once she got out of the hospital and recovered, he had an idea of a joint business venture with her.

Only in your *Wildest Dreams* could someone come back from the dead and confirm that you should never question true love. Just believe in it and keep trying to grow it. Two former enemies united for a common cause and found real friendship out of temporary lust. Sometimes, wildest dreams come true.

The End

Michael Young

www.ingramcontent.com/pod-product-compliance
Lightning Source LLC
Chambersburg PA
CBHW050409030726
47503CB00006B/2110